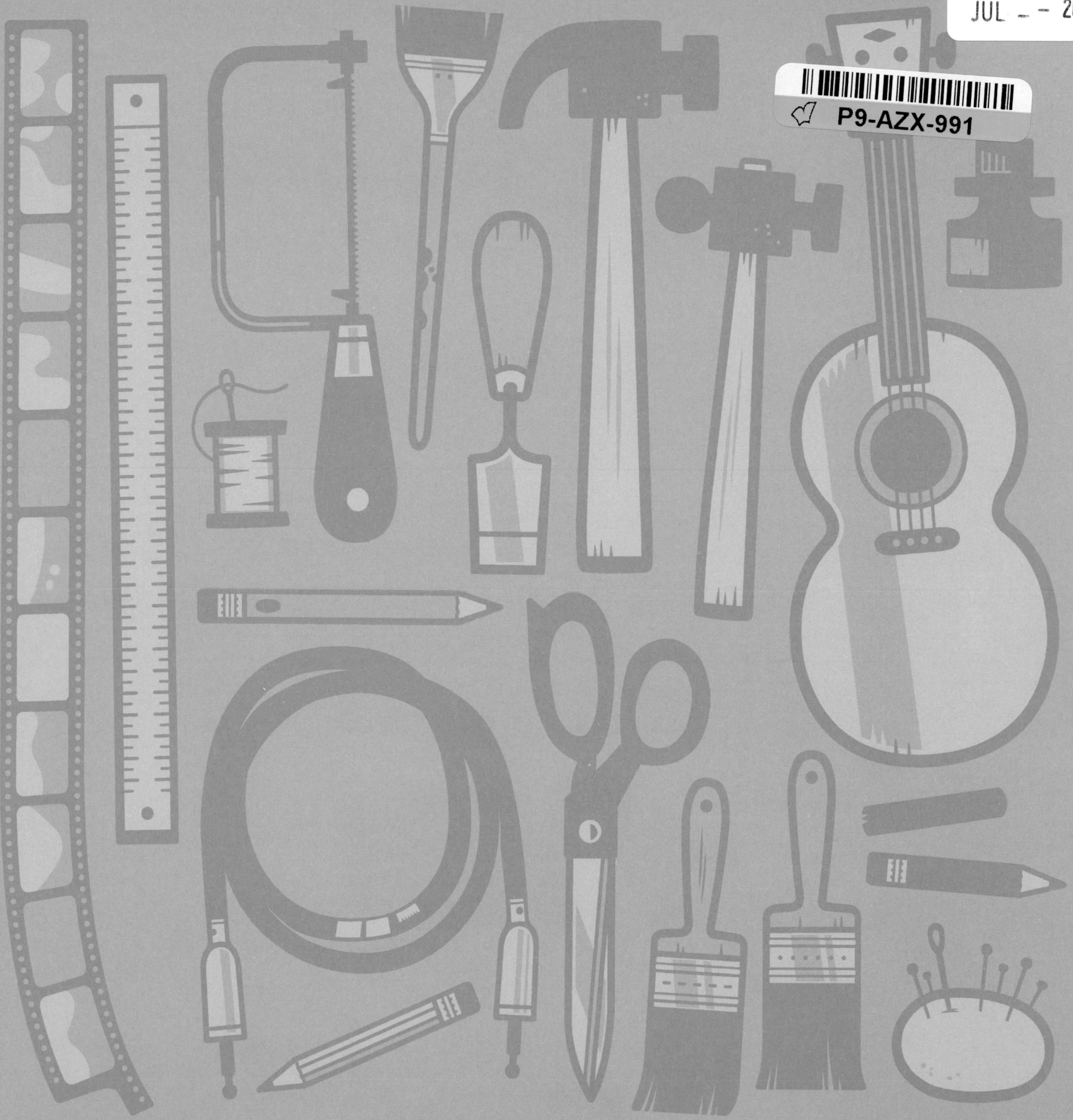

For my studio sister, Danielle Davis
— EA

To Willa and Willowdean
— TLFOP

Tundra Books, an imprint of Penguin Random House Canada Young Readers,
a Penguin Random House Company

Library and Archives Canada Cataloguing in Publication

Title: Studio : a place for art to start / Emily Arrow and The Little Friends of Printmaking.
Names: Arrow, Emily, author. | Little Friends of Printmaking, illustrator.
Identifiers: Canadiana (print) 20190110791 | Canadiana (ebook) 20190121114 |
ISBN 9780735264854 (hardcover) | ISBN 9780735264861 (EPUB)
Classification: LCC PS3601.R563 S78 2020 | DDC j813/.6—dc23

Published simultaneously in the United States of America by Tundra Books of Northern New York,
an imprint of Penguin Random House Canada Young Readers, a Penguin Random House Company

Library of Congress Control Number: 2019941902

Edited by Samantha Swenson
Designed by John Martz
The artwork in this book was created digitally.
The text was set in TT Norms.

Printed and bound in China

www.penguinrandomhouse.ca

1   2   3   4   5   24   23   22   21   20

STUDIO
A PLACE FOR ART TO START

EMILY ARROW

AND

**THE LITTLE FRIENDS
OF PRINTMAKING**

tundra

A place for making music,
A place for making art,
A place to build and dream and move,
A place for art to start.

We call a place a studio
When we're creating in it,

Or practicing, or editing,
Or thinking for a minute.

Some artists need a studio
With lots of room and light.

While others find a tiny nook
Will fit their work just right.

A habitat for makers
With string and sculpting clay;
A place where people twirl and leap
Or simply stop to play.

Perhaps an animator
  Or an actor with a part.
      No matter who, they're free to do
        Whatever's in their hearts.

When we have ideas,
We can bounce them off each other.
Toss them 'round and shake them out;
Make something even better!

And playing with ideas
Can lead to so much more.
I bet you see what's happening:
It's spilling out the door!

From every little studio,
Our tiny magic rooms,
We tell the world our story;
We sing the world our tune.

Art is made for sharing;
An artist always knows
That seeing it a different way
Can help your art to grow.

People in big cities
And teeny tiny towns,
Will hear the joyful melody
Of art that's all around.

Do you have an idea?
Are you ready to create?

Listen to your inner voice
And find your special place.

Finding your own studio
Shouldn't be too hard:
Round the corner, in a park,
Or maybe in your yard.

A place to be creative, wherever that might be.

Make it your own, an artist's home,
A place where you'll be free.